Ja
Again

ANNETTE BUTTERWORTH

ILLUSTRATED BY
NICK BUTTERWORTH

Hodder
Children's
Books

a division of Hodder Headline plc

Text Copyright © Annette Butterworth 1996
Illustrations copyright © Nick Butterworth 1996

First published in Great Britain in 1996 by Hodder Children's Books
This paperback edition first published 1997

The right of Annette Butterworth to be identified
as the Author of the Work and the right of Nick Butterworth
to be identified as the Illustrator has been asserted by them in accordance
with the Copyright, Designs and Patents Act 1988.

10 9 8 7 6 5 4 3 2 1

A Catalogue record for this book is available from the British Library.

ISBN 0 340 68728 2

Printed and bound in Great Britain
by Mackays of Chatham plc, Chatham, Kent

Hodder Children's Books
a division of Hodder Headline PLC
338 Euston Road, London NW1 3BH

*This
book is
dedicated to Nick
with thanks for the pictures
— and all the years of
encouragement.*

A.B.

Chapter One

Jake was in disgrace. It is true he didn't know it was his owner's birthday. But he shouldn't have eaten the whole box of chocolates that was meant to be her birthday present.

When the box arrived on the doormat, Jake thought it was wonderful. Mrs Foster's sister had called and, finding the Fosters out, posted her present through the letter box. But she'd forgotten about Jake. Jake had eaten most of the chocolates, and the ones he didn't like he had left, half chewed and stuck to the carpet. Mr and

Mrs Foster came home to a terrible mess in the hall.

To make matters worse, Jake had dug up some roses that Mr Foster had just planted. They were another present. Mr Foster always sprinkled a handful of bonemeal around the roots of plants to help them grow. Jake hated the smell of roses but he loved bonemeal. So, to get to the bonemeal, he dug up the roses and spoilt Mr Foster's best efforts.

Of course, he was sorry afterwards. Jake always was.

Jake did like having a good dig. He had found some very interesting things, digging. Once, he'd found some old tools that eventually ended up in a museum. Jake wasn't impressed. He'd been hoping to find a bone to eat.

Jake went to the local park with his great friend, Sam, nearly every day. Sam was an old man who lived in a house that backed onto Jake's garden. Sam and the Fosters had become friends through Jake, and Sam took Jake for his daily walks. In the park, they would meet up with their pals; Jake with his doggy friends and Sam with their owners.

Today, Jake crawled through the hole in the fence to Sam's garden. Sam had heard about the chocolates and the roses, but he gave Jake a hug and a pat, and a dog biscuit, as he always did. Sam knew Jake was a dog who tried to be good but sometimes temptations were too much for him.

"Hallo, Jake. You are a rascal," said Sam. "I wonder why you hate roses so much. They're my favourite flowers. I am going to finish my cup of tea and then we'll try out our new football in the park."

Jake was a very good footballer. He was good at dribbling and heading the ball. Football was his favourite game.

"Let's see if I can score a goal today, Jake," said Sam.

Chapter Two

When Jake and Sam arrived at the park, Jake's friends and their owners were at the entrance.

Jake's favourite friend, Holly, a Rough Collie, was there. She lived next door to Jake. Holly had her nephew Harry staying at the moment. Holly and Harry were not as clever as Jake but they were very kind and Harry was very excited to see Jake, who was his hero. Harry wanted to look like Jake when he grew up. Holly didn't like to disappoint him by telling him he wouldn't grow up any further. Holly thought that, anyway, he was quite big enough.

Charles, the Irish Wolfhound, was standing next to his owner, Mr Grant. He gave Jake a friendly nudge. Charles lived on the other side of Jake's garden. To begin with the two had not got on, but now they were firm friends.

The dogs and their owners were gathered reading a poster on the park notice board.

They had very miserable faces.

Mrs Thirkettle, Holly's owner, greeted Sam. "Look, isn't it awful? The Council are going to sell the park!"

"Sell the park! They can't do that, can they?" Sam asked Mr Grant.

"It seems they can," said Mr Grant. "The poster says the park is to become an industrial and business park with factories and office outlets."

"That's terrible," said Sam.

The dogs understood enough to know what the notice meant. Harry wondered if a business park would still be a place where dogs could go. But Jake told him that this sort of park wasn't really a park at all. There would be no grass, no trees, no swings, no bandstand, no tennis courts, no lake, no ducks, no animals at all. And, saddest of all for Jake – no football pitch.

This was dreadful news for the dogs. If they lost their park where else could they run free, without being on a lead? Where would they meet to play their games and exchange stories?

The owners were just as upset.

"What about all the trees?" asked Mrs. Thirkettle. "I've been coming to this park for fifty years and I've seen them grow from saplings to huge, healthy, beautiful trees. They'll pull them all down."

"And there's the lake, of course," said Mr Grant. "All the fish will go, and the geese, ducks, swans, moorhens, coots. And the fishermen will have nowhere. It's just too awful."

"Who are they going to sell the park to?" asked Sam.

"That man over there," said Mr Grant. He pointed to a short fat man smoking a cigar, who was directing some workmen to take measurements.

"What are the Council thinking about?" asked Sam. The fat man with the measuring tape must have overheard. He turned and strolled towards them.

"I'll tell you what they're thinking about," he said, with an unpleasant smile. "Allow me to introduce myself. My name is Ted Griffen and I am the new owner of this park or at least, I will be very soon. The Council want to modernise this town: bring it into the modern age, bring new life to the business community of the area. By selling this park to me, that is exactly what they will be doing."

"And it hasn't got anything to do with the money they will get from the sale?" asked Mr Grant. "Everybody knows they have run out of money."

"That's nothing to do with me," replied Ted Griffen. "I've got a business to run and a living to make and if you don't mind, your dogs are getting in the way of my measuring."

Jake didn't like the man or his measuring. Without any warning, he seized hold of one of the measures and started running round in circles with it, trailing it behind him. Ted Griffen tried to catch him and ended up wrapped in the tape. Everybody was laughing – except Ted Griffen. "You just wait," he shouted. "You won't be laughing soon, when this park belongs to me."

Sam called Jake over and made him let go of the tape. "OK Jakie, that will do. We'll have to think of something else to stop this man," he said.

Sam was very sad. Without the park, there would be no more walks with his great friend Jake, and no more chats with the people there. These were the only friends Sam had. Jake could see Sam was sad. He didn't know how to save the park, but he knew he must.

The dogs and their owners drifted on through the park, but they were not their usual lively selves.

"Of course, you know, the park belongs to the people of the town," said Mrs Thirkettle. "The land was given to us by King Edward the Confessor nearly a thousand years ago! People were allowed to leave their sheep and goats here to graze. There used to be an old piece of sheepskin parchment hanging in the Town Hall. That was the Royal Charter. A very important document. The Charter said that Edward the Confessor gave the land to the town. If it hadn't gone missing, the Council wouldn't be able to sell the park."

"If only we had that Charter," said Mr Grant. "We could prove that the park belongs to the town."

"Well, I haven't seen that Charter since I was a young girl, and that's a long time ago," said Mrs Thirkettle. "But I suppose it must be somewhere."

"Then we must find it," said Sam.

The dogs were trying to understand. Jake didn't know what sheepskin parchment was, but he did know what sheep were. He had seen them on the common. He knew their smell. He thought they needed to find a piece of a sheep. Charles thought perhaps this Charter thing was a special sort of bone and the other dogs agreed. They must find a special sheep's bone and then the park would be safe.

Chapter Three

"I think this public meeting has been arranged much too quickly," Mrs Foster said to Sam. "We haven't had time to think."

They were having their morning cup of tea together after Sam and Jake's walk.

"It's only a week since the Council first put up the board about selling the park."

"That could be their idea," said Sam. "It will be harder for people to stop them if they move fast."

"What did the notice say, Sam?"

"It said that anybody interested should go to the Town Hall tonight for a meeting with the Council, to discuss the sale of the park," Sam replied.

"Such short notice," said Mrs Foster. "Sam, I think I'll take Jake along. Do you think that's a good idea?"

"Wonderful," said Sam, pleased. "Let them meet all the users of the park. And Jake is always full of surprises!"

That evening Sam, Mr and Mrs Foster and Jake arrived at the Town Hall for the public meeting. At first, the doorman refused to let Jake in.

"No dogs," he said gruffly.

"But this isn't just any dog," said Mrs Foster. "This is Jake. The Council have invited 'anybody interested' along to this meeting. And nobody is more interested in the park than Jake!"

"Oh, all right then," said the doorman, reluctantly. "But make sure he behaves himself."

Mr and Mrs Foster, Sam and Jake, found themselves some seats near the back. Mrs Foster looped Jake's lead under a chair leg and they waited for the meeting to begin.

Jake was pleased to find himself sitting behind a little girl. He liked to be made a fuss of. He was even more pleased to see the little girl had some chocolate.

At the front of the hall, on a raised platform, the Councillors sat in a row behind a long table. Ted Griffen, the developer, sat with them. The rest of the hall was packed with townsfolk. The news about the sale of the park had

spread fast and the people of the town were very upset.

"Good evening, ladies and gentlemen. I am Mr Ramsey, the Mayor and Leader of the Council. So good to see so many of you here tonight."

The Mayor, however, didn't look at all pleased to see them. In fact, the Council had hoped to keep the meeting a small and quiet affair.

The Mayor went on to explain that the Council wanted to modernise the town. They wanted to build lots of business facilities to benefit the whole town and

they were sure everybody would gain enormously from the development of the park. The Mayor spoke for ages, boring people with facts and figures.

At last he said, "Are there any questions?"

"Yes," said Mr Grant. "Without the park, where will we be able to get some fresh air and exercise? Our dogs can't run around in the streets, it's not safe. And we'll lose the trees and the lake if you allow this industrial park."

"Well," said the Mayor, "unfortunately, we will have to lose the trees in the park but most people will still be able to walk through the business park."

"And dogs?" asked Mr Foster.

"Oh no, certainly not. No animals allowed in a business park. For health and safety reasons."

"How is the sale of the park going to benefit the ordinary people of the town?" asked Mrs Foster.

"Well," said the Mayor again. He was clearly a bit stuck for an answer and looked at Mr Griffen.

"I'll tell you," interrupted Ted Griffen. "This Council needs more money for schools, roads, and hospitals. The sale of the park will raise this money."

"But why do you need more money?" asked Mrs Foster. "You usually have enough. What's happened to it all?"

"Well," said the Mayor yet again, "we have had to decorate the Council offices and, of course, we had to replace all the councillors' cars."

"The councillors can buy their own cars," said Mr Grant, "and you certainly didn't need to buy those antiques and paintings that you have got in your office."

Jake wasn't interested in what the Mayor had to say. He and the little girl had finished the chocolate ages ago. Now they were bored. They watched as a bee lazily buzzed between the chairs.

Jake lowered his head onto his paws, and sighed.

"It isn't right," said Mrs Thirkettle. "That park belongs to the people of this town. It was given to us by Edward the Confessor nearly a thousand years ago, by Royal Charter. The Charter used to be here, in the Town Hall. It gave the parkland to us, and it isn't the Council's to sell."

"Ah yes, well," said the Mayor, "that is a very old story and nobody has seen that 'Charter', if it ever existed, for years and years. If it were to be found, which is highly unlikely, we would, of course, abide by it. In the meantime, however, the Council takes the view that the park should be sold. For the benefit of the town, of course. I think we all agree then," he said, looking at the other councillors, "that unless we have another offer, we should accept Mr Griffen's generous one and sell the park to him."

Everybody, except the councillors, began to boo the Mayor. At this point, the bee buzzed past Jake's nose. He couldn't resist it. He jumped up and rushed after it, snapping at it, trying to catch it. Unfortunately, the chair, with his lead wrapped around it, went with him. Mr Foster fell onto the floor and Jake knocked over several other chairs.

Suddenly, the meeting was in uproar. People hurried to get out of Jake's way. As the bee flew past the Mayor, Jake rushed past him, knocked him over and finally caught the bee.

"Er, I think I'd better declare the meeting over," the Mayor yelled from the floor.

"Oh Jake," said Mrs Foster, as she got hold of his lead. "Why are you always so naughty?"

"But it was funny, wasn't it, to see the Mayor on the floor?" Sam laughed.

Jake was sorry that he'd pulled Mr Foster over. He had got carried away by the bee. He had to admit that he wasn't very sorry he'd knocked the Mayor over.

Chapter Four

After the meeting at the Town Hall, the people of the town knew they had to find a way to save the park.

The councillors, and especially the Mayor, were determined to sell it. They all wanted to keep their new cars. And the Mayor had taken a particular dislike to Jake.

At first, they tried to find the missing Charter. If it could be found, the park couldn't be sold.

Mr and Mrs Foster, and Sam, went to the local library to see if it was kept there. There was no sign of it. But a helpful librarian told them that Mrs Thirkettle was right. King Edward *had* given the park to the town.

Mrs Foster then wrote to several big museums in London, to see if any of them had the Charter or knew where it was. But none of them could help. She spent a whole day in one museum and found nothing.

She did wonder if the Queen knew about the Charter. After all, she must be related to King Edward. So she wrote to the Queen to ask if she had the Charter.

Mrs Foster received a letter back from her Majesty saying that she was very sorry, she had looked everywhere she could think, but she couldn't find the Charter either. She very much hoped that it would turn up in time to save the park.

"What are we going to do?" Mrs Foster said to Sam. "We can't save the park without that Charter. It must be somewhere. But where? Suppose somebody has destroyed it!"

"Don't give up hope, Mrs Foster," said Sam. "Something might turn up."

The next morning, Jake and Sam arrived at the park as usual, to find Ted Griffen and his workmen already there. They were busy, drawing up plans and painting white crosses on a group of trees which were roped off to stop people getting near them.

"The Council are letting these people cut down some trees to make room for their machines. They don't even own the park yet but they're so sure they will!" Mrs Thirkettle said. Sam knew that Mrs

Thirkettle was very fond of this group of trees.

Jake watched in horror as a workman took a large chainsaw and attacked one of the big trees.

There was a crowd of people watching and shouting. The dogs joined in by barking loudly.

"Now, stand well back, for your own safety," said Ted Griffen. "We can't cut trees down with people too close."

Sam was suddenly very angry. "You shouldn't be cutting them down at all," he shouted, and he gave Jake's football a mighty kick.

Jake thought it was time for a game. He chased after it, and began to dribble it in and out of the big oaks. He got completely in the way of the workmen.

"Call your dog off," shouted Griffen. But Sam stayed silent. He watched with

amusement. The other owners allowed the rest of the dogs to join in the fun. It was impossible for the workmen to carry on. They couldn't cut trees down with dogs running around them, so they had to give up.

"You wait!" shouted Ted Griffen. "You think you've stopped us. But you haven't. When this park belongs to me, there'll be a big sign on that gate that says 'Keep Out'. And that'll mean you." He pointed at the dogs and glared at Jake in particular.

The workmen packed up all their equipment and left the park.

"He's right of course," said Mr Grant. "We've won today but he'll be back. We have to find a way of stopping that man."

After supper that night, Jake pushed through the fence to Sam's garden. Sam was enjoying a cup of tea in the garden before he turned in for the night.

"Hallo Jake. Well, old boy, what are we going to do? Where am I going to take you to play football? It looks like we're going to lose the park."

"Not if I can help it," thought Jake. "There must be something I can do."

Chapter Five

Next day, Sam went to visit Mr and Mrs Foster. As the Charter could not be found, they needed to find another way of saving the park.

"I wonder how much the park is being sold for," said Mrs Foster. "Perhaps the people of the town could raise the money and buy it, instead of Ted Griffen."

"Well," said Mr Foster, "we would be buying something that already belongs to us. But if it's the only way to save the park, then perhaps we should try."

Mrs Foster telephoned the Town Hall to find out just how much money the park was being sold for. She was surprised to hear that it was less than she thought. The Council needed money quickly. She was told that if the townsfolk could pay as much as Ted Griffen, they could buy the park it would be saved.

"Then there's hope," said Sam.

"It's still a lot of money to find," said Mr Foster.

"I know," said Mrs Foster, "but we must try. We need to get some people together and think of ideas. I'll start up a fund-raising committee at once. We haven't any time to lose."

Mrs Foster organised a meeting for everybody interested in saving the park. The Fosters' house was packed out. Jake loved it. He liked meeting new people.

People came up with lots of ideas. There would be a sponsored walk, a fun run and a sponsored swim. Jake liked the sound of the walk and the fun run but he wasn't keen on the swim. It seemed too much like a bath.

Mr Grant was put in charge of writing to local businesses to ask them for money. They wouldn't want big, new businesses opening near them.

The main event would be a Grand Fair. There would be lots of side shows and attractions. They would ask the Council's permission to hold the Fair in the park.

The next few weeks were very busy. There were lots of preparations to be made.

First there was the sponsored walk. Walkers asked to be sponsored in two ways. They would be paid for the distance they walked and they would be paid for each leg. All the dogs joined in. As they had four legs instead of two, they raised more money than the humans.

The sponsored fun run took place in the park. Owners and dogs ran together. Sam provided the drinks for the runners. Jake didn't always run in the right direction because there were so many squirrels and rabbits to chase, but he did have fun.

Organising the Fair was a very big job. There needed to be lots of things for people to spend their money on. The park would be full of attractions, things to do and goodies to buy and eat. Posters were put up all round the town to advertise it.

The day before the Fair, everybody was hard at work preparing. They put up flags and balloons and laid out all the stalls and attractions.

"Let's hope we have good weather tomorrow," said Mrs Thirkettle. "We've done all we can."

Chapter Six

The day of the Fair dawned. A few early clouds soon cleared. It was going to be a lovely sunny day. Everyone was relieved. They hoped that all their hard work would be rewarded.

Mr and Mrs Foster and Sam arrived at the park early. Before the Fair started, Jake was allowed to wander round by himself, looking at all the attractions.

In one corner, there was a small fun fair, with a carousel of painted horses, a big wheel and a helter skelter.

On the lake, there were remote control

boats. The ducks were not too sure about them and retreated to the safety of the reeds.

Jake liked the look of the cake stall. He would visit that later!

There were two bouncy castles. Jake tried to have a bounce on one but was chased off because of his sharp claws.

Soon it was time to open the park gates so that the Fair could begin. Mrs Thirkettle cut the red ribbon stretched across the entrance, the local brass band began to play and the fun started.

By the gates there was a shooting range and a coconut shy and next to that, a crockery smash. Jake wondered why it was that people were allowed to make such an awful mess. He was always being told off for breaking much less.

There was lots of food to eat. Candy floss and toffee apples were on sale. Jake tried some candy floss that had fallen off a stick. Unusually for Jake, he thought it was too sweet and it got wrapped round his teeth. But he did like a toffee apple that a little boy gave him.

There was a hot dog and burger stall. This was popular, especially with the

dogs, who were very quick to pick up any dropped burgers. Jake went back to the cake stall. He'd noticed there was a whole tray of home-made chocolates on it. When nobody was looking, he nudged the tray and the chocolates fell on the ground. They were delicious!

Mr Grant had set himself up as a human jukebox. He stood inside a big cardboard box, painted to look like a jukebox. Pasted onto the front was a long list of songs which he could sing. People paid him to sing the song of their choice. Mr Grant's singing was enthusiastic but Mr Foster, on the next stall, wished it was slightly more tuneful. After listening to Mr Grant's efforts for nearly an hour, he paid him to be quiet for five minutes' peace.

Because of his footballing skills, Jake was given a stall to himself. Mr Foster had set up goal posts and measured out an area where people could shoot. Sam held Jake until Mr Foster said "Go", then the competitor tried to score a goal past Jake. Amazingly, only one goal was scored and that was by a little boy who had dropped his ice cream just as he was going to shoot. Instead of going for the ball, Jake went for the ice cream. Jake was kept busy all afternoon. He was exhausted by the end but he'd raised a lot of money and thoroughly enjoyed himself.

All the dogs from the park played their part. A Bernese Mountain dog was harnessed to a little cart and spent the afternoon giving children rides. Charles marched up and down in his father's regimental regalia and collected donations of money in a pot strapped to his back. Even Holly and Harry did their party piece: they shook hands with people.

At the end of the day, Mr and Mrs Foster and Sam counted the money. They had all the money from the Fair, collections, sponsored events and some very generous donations from local businesses, but they were dismayed to find that they still didn't have enough money to buy the park.

There was one last chance. Mr Grant said that one business in the town, Technicom, might give them the amount they needed. But their directors had still not decided.

Everybody was very worried. Even after all their hard work they might not manage to meet the Council's deadline. They only had another couple of days left.

Next day, Sam and the Fosters talked about the problem.

"We haven't raised enough money so,

at the moment, there is nothing to stop Ted Griffen buying the park on Monday. That means tomorrow's the last day we can visit the park." said Mr Foster. "Sam, we'd like to come with you and Jake tomorrow. It'll be the last time for all of us."

Tears welled up in Sam's eyes. "I don't like to think about it," he said. "A walk in the park with Jake is the highlight of my day."

Jake sat next to Sam and gently put his paw on Sam's knee. Even if they couldn't go to the park together, Sam would always be Jake's favourite person.

Chapter Seven

Next day, Mr and Mrs Foster, Sam, Mrs Thirkettle, Jake, Holly and Harry set out for the park together.

When they arrived, they were dismayed to find that the park had already been closed off to the public, and the lovely old park gates were barricaded. Angry locals were gathered around the entrance and all the dogs were looking very agitated.

Fierce-looking barbed wire and steel

reinforced the barricades on top ne park fence.

"This is disgraceful," said Mr Grant. "The park won't be sold until tomorrow. They've no right to do this."

"Yes, this is very unfair. The park still belongs to the town until tomorrow," said Mr Foster.

The portly figure of Ted Griffen appeared behind the barricades.

"Ladies and gentlemen, the Council has given permission for the site to be prepared today, so that construction can start tomorrow," he said.

"It's not a site, it's our park!" shouted Sam.

"That's tough," said Ted Griffen. "Let's face it. You've lost. There's no Charter, the park is mine now, and there's nothing you can do about it."

Sam and Jake turned away from the

park gates for the last time.

"Well, boy, we'll just have to walk on the common," Sam said, and the other dogs and their owners joined them.

Jake knew what this meant. He would have to stay on the lead and not be allowed to run free. There were sheep on the common. Dogs had to be kept on leads. They certainly couldn't play football.

The smell of the sheep on the common reminded Jake of the sheep's bone he thought they were looking for, which would save the park.

"It's a pity that Charter bone thing hasn't turned up. Who would have thought a bone could make so much difference?" Jake thought to himself.

Everybody went home feeling very sad. Their last trip to the park had been ruined.

"Well, that's it." said Mr Foster. "We haven't enough money to buy the park, so now it is lost."

Chapter Eight

On Monday, Jake was woken very early by the telephone ringing.

Mrs Foster answered it. "Yes, that's right," she said. "Yes. Really? Well that's wonderful news, thanks so much for letting me know so quickly. Yes, we'll meet you at the Town Hall at ten o'clock."

Mrs Foster put the telephone back and told Mr Foster about the message. Mr

Grant had telephoned. Technicom had sent him a cheque for the rest of the money they needed. Now they could offer as much money as Ted Griffen. The townsfolk could buy the park after all!

Jake rushed out to tell Holly, Harry and Charles.

Everyone was feeling very excited.

The Fosters, Sam and Mrs Thirkettle gathered all the money together. The deadline was eleven o'clock, so they were going to the Town Hall an hour early to give the Council the money. To his disgust, Jake was brushed thoroughly and made to look smart.

"Have to look your best for the presentation, Jake," said Mrs Foster, trying to make him keep still. "Now, stand up, Jake, I can't brush you lying down."

When they were ready, Jake, Sam, the

Fosters and Mrs Thirkettle walked to the Town Hall. Mr Grant was waiting for them and handed over the money from Technicom.

Ted Griffen was also waiting to see the Mayor. He was shown into the Mayor's office first.

After a short time, Jake's group were asked into the office. The Mayor was standing with Ted Griffen, who was wearing a smug grin.

The Mayor's office was very large and lavishly decorated. The furniture looked new and expensive with several beautiful paintings hanging on the walls. In pride of place, there was a large and very old painting of the park, showing the beautiful trees that Ted Griffen's men were now cutting down.

Mrs Foster stepped forward. "Mr Mayor, I'm very pleased to tell you that the people of the town have managed to raise the same amount as Mr Griffen, and so, on their behalf, I'd like to make an offer to buy the park," she said.

For an awkward moment, the Mayor was silent. "Oh dear," he said at last. "Oh dear, you see, I'm afraid that's not possible."

Mrs Foster looked puzzled. "Why ever not?" she said. "You told us that the Council would sell the park to us if we raised as much as Ted Griffen has offered."

"Well, that's just it, I'm afraid," said the Mayor. "Mr Griffen has just offered me twice as much as before. My duty to the Council is to sell the park to the highest bidder."

"What about your duty to the people of the town?" shouted Mr Grant. "This is outrageous!"

Everybody started shouting. The Mayor panicked and called for his security guards to throw them all out.

"You can't do this," said Mr Foster. "You must listen to us. It's our park." And he began to struggle with a security guard who had taken hold of his arm.

Suddenly, things happened very quickly. A table was knocked over, which sent a large pot plant flying. As the plant fell, it knocked the painting of the park off the wall. The painting crashed onto a filing cabinet and ended up on the floor. The frame was damaged and the canvas was ripped open.

"Now look what you've done!" shouted the Mayor. "That painting is extremely valuable, more valuable than you could possibly know." He rushed to get hold of the painting but Jake got there first.

Jake scratched at the ripped canvas and made it even worse. "Look at what your dreadful dog is doing," yelled the Mayor. "Stop him. He's ruining the painting."

Everybody was horrified. Jake was scratching away frantically.

"Oh Jake," Mrs Foster cried. "What are you doing?"

Sam went to stop Jake, who was, by

now, tearing furiously at the painting. Then something caught Sam's eye. Something was stuck between the canvas and the back of the painting.

Sam looked closer. "All right boy, I can see it. I'll get it now," Sam said to Jake. Carefully he took hold of the painting and out slid an old brown document.

"So, what is this?" he said. He handed it to Mrs Thirkettle. She stared at it for a moment. Then a huge smile spread over her face.

"This, everyone, is the Royal Charter," she said, "which gives the parkland to the people of this town 'in perpetuity'. That means for ever. It says here that the land must always be a park for the town 'by order of King Edward'."

"Hurrah!" said Mrs Foster. "So the park isn't yours to sell," she said to the

Mayor, "and you can't buy it!" she said to Ted Griffen.

"Just a minute," said Mr Grant, "I hope you didn't know the Charter was in that painting, Mr Mayor."

The Mayor just sat red-faced at his desk, his eyes bulging, unable to speak.

"Well done, Jake!" said Sam. "You've saved the day. I think you could smell the Charter, couldn't you boy?"

"Yes, well done, Jake!" said Mrs Foster. "What a good job you came with us." And everybody, except the Mayor and Ted Griffen, made a big fuss of Jake.

As soon as the painting had ripped, Jake recognised the smell. It was the same as the sheep on the common.

"Sheepskin, not sheep's bone!" thought Jake.

Chapter Nine

Thanks to Jake, the park was safe. The Charter was put in a very secure place by the townsfolk in a vault in the main bank. Ted Griffen and his men were made to take down the barricades at the park and plant new trees for any they had cut down. The councillors were dismissed and made to sell their cars. The rest of the paintings and the antiques were sold.

The townsfolk used the money they had raised to improve the park. They planted some more trees, put in new swings and roundabouts, renovated the bandstand and did many of the jobs the Council should have done but hadn't.

There was still some money left, so, to celebrate, they held a slap-up picnic in the park, in Jake's honour.

Jake had a wonderful time. There were lots of games to play and food to eat, including a cake made out of chocolate.

Best of all, Jake was allowed to play football with the local team on the big football pitch.

Tired but happy, Jake walked home with Sam and the gang.

"Jake," said Sam, "thanks to you, one

of my favourite places has been saved. Thank you." And he gave Jake a big hug.

That night, Jake was pottering around the garden when he smelt it. Bonemeal. Mr Foster had planted some bulbs, and he had used bonemeal.

Jake was about to dig them up, when a voice called out behind him. "Jake, what are you doing?" Mr Foster was standing at the back door.

Jake turned and trotted back to the house.

"Just checking," he said to himself.

A GIFT FROM WINKLESEA

Helen Cresswell

A trip to the seaside changes Dan and Mary's lives forever.

The gift they bring back for their mother couldn't be more perfect – a beautiful bluish egg-shaped stone with gold lettering. They put it on the mantelpiece for everyone to admire.

And there it stays. Until Mary notices something strange about it – it feels warm to the touch – and sure enough, one day – it hatches . . .

JAKE

Annette Butterworth
Illustrated by Nick Butterworth

Jake loves to chase ducks in the park, can't resist playing with dirty washing and no chocolate eggs are safe with him around!

He dreams of going to Crufts, the biggest and best dog show in the world. But he knows he'll never get there . . .

But Jake is a very special dog. He's not just good at football, he's the best friend you could ever have — and sometimes even a dog's dream can come true!

ORDER FORM

0 340 66749 4	JAKE *Annette Butterworth*	£2.99 ☐
0 340 10472 4	A GIFT FROM WINKLESEA *Helen Cresswell (hardback)*	£8.99 ☐
0 340 64648 9	WHATEVER HAPPENED IN WINKLESEA? *Helen Cresswell (hardback)*	£8.99 ☐
0 340 64649 7	MYSTERY AT WINKLESEA *Helen Cresswell (hardback)*	£8.99 ☐
0 340 61954 6	HAMISH *W. J. Corbett*	£2.99 ☐
0 340 62653 4	PRINCE VINCE AND THE CASE OF THE SMELLY GOAT *Valerie Wilding*	£2.99 ☐
0 340 62654 2	PRINCE VINCE AND THE HOT DIGGORY DOGS *Valerie Wilding*	£2.99 ☐

All Hodder Children's Books are available at your local bookshop or newsagent, or can be ordered direct from the publisher. Just tick the titles you want and fill in the form below. Prices and availability subject to change without notice.

Hodder Children's Books, Cash Sales Department, Bookpoint, 39 Milton Park, Abingdon, OXON, OX14 4TD, UK. If you have a credit card you may order by telephone – (01235) 831700.

Please enclose a cheque or postal order made payable to Bookpoint Ltd to the value of the cover price and allow the following for postage and packing:
UK and BFPO – £1.00 for the first book, 50p for the second book, and 30p for each additional book ordered up to a maximum charge of £3.00.
OVERSEAS AND EIRE – £2.00 for the first book, £1.00 for the second book, and 50p for each additional book.

OR Please debit this amount from my Access/Visa Card (delete as appropriate)

Card Number | | | | | | | | | | | | | | | | |

Amount £ ....

Expiry Date ....

Signed ....

Name ....

Address ....

....